Attention! Attention! It is time for you to meet Lilah Dill, a fearless seven year old who was born to perform. Following in the footsteps of her daddy and her Nana Belle, Lilah can sing and dance but is ready for a new act. More than anything, she dreams of performing magic on stage as Shagundula the magician.

Read on to see what tricks she may have up her sleeve. One thing is for sure...you'll be in for a magical time.

Lilah Dill and the Magic Kit

BY JL JUSAITIS

ILLUSTRATED BY

EDYTHA RYAN

LILAH DILL AND THE MAGIC KIT
© 2012 by JL Jusaitis

Illustrations by Edytha Ryan

Book design by Jo-Anne Rosen

ISBN 978-1478336495

Swan Lake Books
Petaluma, California

Printed in the U.S.A. by createspace.com

To

Little Nana

Contents

Lilah Dill and
the Magic Kit

CHAPTER ONE

Meet Lilah Dill

Delilah Dilitis stood in front of her mama's big round mirror. "Delilah is a giant super-star—just ask anyone," she shouted. "I'll prove it to you." She spun a perfect pirouette, finishing with a deep bow. "Just call me Lilah Dill. That's my stage name." She winked at the perky girl in the mirror, and the mirror girl winked back.

"Delilah, what are you doing?" her mama called from the kitchen of their long California house.

"Nothing," Lilah sang, in her attempt at a high soprano opera-lady voice.

Her daddy, Darius Dilitis, appeared at the bedroom door, singing. "I think that she wants you to help with the din-ner." His booming baritone voice rattled the perfume bottles. He continued the song with "because even us show-offs need to help with the din-ner."

"The din-ner," Lilah sang.

"Yes, the din-ner."

"The dinner, dinner, dinner, din-ner." Lilah and her daddy sang this last line as a duet, and ended it by striking a pose. They held their pose, arms extended, admiring the statue of the two opera singers in the mirror. Dinner was forgotten.

Lilah's little twin brothers, Bongo and Jonny-cake, came running into the bedroom and screeched to a stop. Sergeant Pepper, their parakeet, sat on Bongo's shoulder while Jonny-cake carried their old cat, Buster, in his arms. They posed too, joining the statues in the mirror.

"Delilah, Bongo, Jonny-cake," called Polly Dilitis. "Come set the table, dinner's almost ready."

The opera troupe in the mirror broke their pose and marched out of the bedroom, to dinner.

~

Dinner a distant memory, Lilah's mama, Polly, stood at the kitchen sink washing a sweater by hand.

"Mama," Lilah said, "more than anything I want a magic kit for my birthday."

"Yes I know," her mama said, "Now, you do know that there's really no such thing as magic, don't you? A magic kit is just a box of tricks."

"I know, but I want a magic wand and a cape and a top hat, and I want to fool people and make them think that I can do magic."

Lilah stepped into a handstand and balanced up against the kitchen counter. "I think I will call myself Lilah the Magnificent, or maybe Shagundala, Woman of Mystery."

Her mama, still standing at the sink, looked taller from this angle, and when Mama talked, Lilah could see the roof of her mouth.

"I've wanted to be a magician ever since I can remember," Lilah said.

"We'll see," Mama said. Lilah thought that Mama's nose holes looked particularly large.

Mama wiped her hands with the dish-cloth and smiled at Lilah. "Sweetie, a good magic kit is hard to find and could be very expensive. I don't want you getting your hopes too high, and besides, a birthday present is suppose to be a surprise. Meanwhile, would you please clear a spot for this sweater on the laundry room table?"

Shagundula, Woman of Mystery, dismounted, Olympic style, with both hands in the air and skipped off to the laundry. "Okie dokie, but I'm really wishing hard for one."

CHAPTER TWO

Happy Birthday

Lilah's father hosted a radio talk show in the mornings, called the Darius Dill Show. The radio show thought that his last name was too long, so they asked him to shorten it. He'd been Darius Dill for so long that even Lilah thought that it was his real name. He only worked in the mornings, so that gave him plenty of time to get the backyard ready for her seventh birthday party.

Lilah planned her party very carefully—it would be an outdoor karaoke party on the lanai, so that she could use the small outdoor stage. In her town, everyone said "lanai" instead of "patio" or "deck." That's because the sugar company, where lots of people worked, got their sugar cane from Hawaii. Lanai was a Hawaiian word.

Lilah and her daddy made up a little song and dance act. At the party, they would wear tuxedos and twirl black canes with white tips. Lilah thought that a tuxedo looked a lot like a magician's costume, so she'd be ready, just in case. She could count on her daddy's best friend, Cornball Cloke, to be there to help with the music and microphone.

She couldn't wait to see Nana Belle, her mama's mama, who was coming to her party. Then there were her two best friends, Jilly and Ruthie. And of course, Bongo and Jonny-cake and her mother's three best friends, the Chicks, would be there too. Those were the important guests.

Also coming to the party were some other girls from Lilah's ballet class and a couple of kids from the neighborhood. In all, a dozen or more people would be there to enjoy the show, eat hamburgers and birthday cake, sing karaoke and see Lilah open her magic kit, she hoped.

On the day of the party, Lilah woke up to loud music blasting out of the speakers by her bed. Her mother, father and the twins were singing a Beatles song at the top of their lungs. "They say it's your birthday, happy birthday to you."

Lilah pulled the covers up over her head and they all jumped on her bed, tickling her until she got up. *Yep,* she thought, *it's officially my birthday.*

"Crispy orange pancakes for breakfast!" her mama said. "Last one to the table is a rotten egg." They all raced to the table and her daddy was the rotten egg. Sun streamed through the windows as Lilah poured syrup on her steaming pancakes, but she noticed a few clouds over the distant hills.

"I hope it won't rain for my party," she said. "The lanai's all ready to go."

Daddy speared a piece of sausage with his fork. "No problem. It's going to be sunny, but if we have to we can move inside. The barbeque is under the eaves so I can still cook."

"But what about our act?"

"Improvise, my dear. That's show biz."

Lilah smiled at her father. He knew show biz up and down. He had a comedy act where he lip-synced operas and funny songs. Also, he owned lots of costumes and props.

Lilah looked at her mother who was coming back from the kitchen with more pancakes, and thought about how lucky she was to have such a great mama. Not only was Mama fun, but she could make wonderful costumes—when she wasn't working for the sugar company.

Lilah looked out the window and saw that the cloud was getting darker and coming closer.

CHAPTER **THREE**

Me and My Shadow

Lilah stood at the door and greeted each guest as they arrived. After lots of practice, her welcome speech sounded grown up and professional. "Welcome to my birthday party. I'm so glad you could come. Please place your gift on the table and find a seat in the back yard."

Lilah's tuxedo collar was itchy, so she scratched her neck as she gave the dark cloud another look. Where were Mama and Nana Belle?

Finally, Nana Belle made her grand entrance. She turned up twenty-five minutes late, with Lilah waiting, looking up and down the street the whole time. Nana Belle wore a pink flowing dress covered in sparkles, pink earrings, pink bracelets, a pink necklace and she even wore pink shoes.

"Here I am," she said, "and I'm in the pink!" Nana Belle didn't have a gift with her but Lilah pretended that she didn't notice.

"Oh Nana. You're just in time for the show. I've been waiting and waiting," said Lilah.

Nana gave her a big hug and a pink lipsticked kiss. "You know I'd never miss one of your shows, Delilah. . . especially on your birthday. Now, where are my little boys?" She rushed off to the back yard.

After wiping Nana's lipstick off her face, Lilah snuck out the back door so that she could enter the stage from behind a hedge. Darius was waiting for her with her top hat and cane and Cornball hid behind the tool shed with the stereo. She peeked through a hole in the hedge and could see her friends, Jilly and Ruthie in the front row. They were sitting up straight with their hands folded on their laps, ready for the performance. Lilah gave Cornball the thumbs up signal and he pushed the button for a trumpet fanfare. That was her cue.

Lilah walked out to center stage, her tap shoes making a klackety-racket. She could see that they had what her daddy called "a full house." Every chair was taken and a few people stood in the back.

Nana Belle gave her a big wave.

"Ladies and Gentlemen" Lilah began. "Thank you for coming to the celebration of my seventh birthday. For today's entertainment, Darius Dill, of the Darius Dill Radio Show and myself, Lilah Dill, will perform our rendition of an old song called Me and My Shadow." At this point, Darius came out on stage and took his position. The audience began clapping. Lilah put her hand up to quiet them. "Please hold your applause until we have finished, and then, if you happen to be standing, we will appreciate an ovation."

She thought she saw her mama snicker in the back. Lilah's daddy gave her that last line and she was quite proud of it. Polly was sitting with The Chicks while Bongo and Jonny-cake sat on the grass in front of the front row, eyes squinting in the sun and mouths open. Their pointy hair made them look like two pineapples sitting side by side.

Now Lilah rapped her cane on the stage and Cornball hit the play button. Darius started the song and dance and Lilah played his shadow. They switched parts for the second verse. She and her daddy danced in perfect sync. They both took off their hats and twirled their canes at exactly the same time. Their days of practice had paid off. Lilah performed a tap solo for the third verse and then she and Darius sang a duet for the last verse, ending arm in arm, kicking high kicks together with the beat.

The audience jumped to their feet, giving them a standing ovation while Lilah and Darius took their bows. Lilah's daddy gave her a wink and a smile and her heart soared. This was the best birthday ever.

But just as she was thinking of a possible encore, a big clap of thunder rolled through the skies, and bathtubs of rain came pouring down onto her party. Everyone grabbed their drinks and belongings and ran into the house *wiki wiki*. That meant "very quickly" in Hawaiian.

What a disappointment! They hadn't even gotten to the karaoke and water was running off the tails of Lilah's tux. Well, the show must go on.

CHAPTER FOUR

Rain, Rain, Go Away

By the time Lilah got into the house she could already hear Nana Belle at the piano. Once Nana Belle got started, nobody could stop her—and really nobody wanted to except for Lilah's daddy. He liked to be the star.

Lilah could see her daddy talking to Cornball Cloke who held the karaoke machine. She had planned on her father being the MC for the karaoke contest. MC means Master of Ceremonies and Darius

Dill was very good at that.

First Nana played very very old sing-a-long songs. Luckily, she had pages with the words so that everyone could sing. Then, unluckily, she started in on the war protest songs. She loved them. By the time they got to "Where Have All The Flowers Gone" everyone had gotten very sad. The saddest person was Lilah.

Lilah was sad for the dead soldiers in the song, but she was also sad for her very sad birthday party. It was getting worse and worse. Bongo let Sergeant Pepper out of his cage and half of the people were looking for a red and green parakeet. The other half went off looking for Buster the cat. Nana still sang, loud and clear.

Ruthie and Jilly stuck close to Lilah, trying to keep her spirits up.

"Girlfriend, you and your daddy were amazing," said Ruthie.

Ruthie had been calling her "Girlfriend" ever since she saw some lady call her friends that on Nickelodeon.

"Yes," Jilly said. "Everybody is talking about it. You guys are so good that you could be on T.V."

"Really? You really think we were that good or are you just trying to make me feel better?"

Together, Ruthie and Jilly said, "That's what friends are for." Lilah laughed. Maybe this party could still be a success.

Clang, Clang, Clang. Lilah's daddy was striking the big iron dinner bell out on the lanai. "Come and get it," he yelled. "Lunch is ready."

Polly and the Chicks had decorated

the table in black and white and silver. A frosting painting of Lilah in her tuxedo decorated the cake. There were seven candles, each one a different color. All of the other food circled the table, so people could admire the cake as they dished up their lunch.

Meanwhile, the twins found Sergeant Pepper and Buster, and locked them up in their cage and laundry room, respectively. Things were back under control and everybody looked like they were having a good time. *My party's getting wonderful again,* Lilah thought.

Cornball Cloke came up to Lilah to ask her if she'd like him to hook up the karaoke machine for singing, but Polly jumped in and said, "No, I think Nana Belle wore everybody's vocal chords out.

It's time for some cake. Delilah, come blow out the candles and then you can open your presents." Lilah could see her daddy lighting the seventh candle.

Lilah looked at her beautiful birthday cake with the glowing candles while everyone sang "Happy Birthday." Right before blowing out the candles she made a wish. She looked up at her mama and her mama gave her a wink and a smile. She took in a deep breath and blew. Six candles went out but one stubborn flame remained. Lilah gave it another quick blow and the last candle went out. She hoped that the extra blow didn't affect her wish.

Lilah cut the first piece of cake and made sure that it was a corner piece with lots of frosting.

"Good job, Lilah" said Mama. "We can take over with the cutting so that you can eat your cake. When everyone's finished with their cake you may open your presents."

After what seemed a really long time, Lilah sat on the floor with her colorful stack of presents. Ruthie and Jilly sat on either side. Lilah opened each present with as much care as she could, then handed the paper to Ruthie, who folded it carefully. Ruthie liked arts and crafts. "You never know when some wrapping paper might come in handy," she said.

The first present that Lilah opened was a stuffed animal from Jilly and Ruthie, who knew that she had always wanted a dog. Lilah hugged her new cocker spaniel, petting his soft coat, and thought that he was almost as good as a real dog. Next she opened a book, and then a set of colored pencils and then several other presents. She made sure that she thanked each and every person as she admired each gift.

Finally it was time to open the last present, the one from her parents. It was medium sized and elaborately wrapped in foil and a huge bow. The present was hard for Lilah to open, with her fingers crossed for good luck. The box was full of tissue paper, but then way down on the bottom, she saw a blue velvet box. Lilah opened the box to find a lovely silver charm bracelet inside. The silver chain sparkled quite brilliantly with three silver charms—a music note, a ballet slipper, and a black top hat.

Disappointed, she fought for a smile as she thanked her parents. Jilly's eyes got all squinty as she worked the clasp and put it on Lilah's wrist. Lilah really did love the bracelet. It was very pretty and fit just right. It just wasn't what she really wanted the most. She sighed and then blushed, feeling ashamed of her greediness. She didn't want to hurt her parent's feelings.

"What's under the piano?" shouted Bongo. His voice sounded very stiff, like he had rehearsed his line.

"It looks like a present!" shouted Jonny-cake, in the same rehearsed way. He threw his hands up in an exaggerated act of surprise.

On cue, Nana Belle said, "Oh! I forgot! You haven't opened my present yet, Lilah."

CHAPTER FIVE

A Magical Present

Nana's "forgotten" present, under the piano, was wrapped in paper decorated with hats and rabbits, and was tied with a big red bow. Could it be? Lilah's hopes began to soar. The twins pulled out the present from under the piano and delivered it to Lilah, while Nana beamed.

Lilah pulled at the red ribbon to remove the bow and then she carefully unwrapped the paper. Ruthie folded the paper, biting her lip with concentration as she smoothed the creases.

"Wiki wiki, Lilah," said Jilly. "You're making us crazy with this!"

Now that the paper had been removed they could read the big yellow letters on a blue box that read "SHAZAM," and then, in smaller letters that read: "the magician's first tool kit." Crescent moons and stars covered the rest of the box.

Lilah's hands shook so hard that she could barely open it. Inside was a bright red fake alligator-skin suitcase with a gold lock, the key taped to the top. SHAZAM was tooled into the skin. It looked even more wonderful than she had imagined.

She looked up at her Nana Belle. "Thank you so much, Nana. You always know what I want." She jumped up, threw her arms around Nana Belle and gave her a loud kiss on the cheek. Nana's plump arms hugged her back.

Lilah sat back down on the floor and rubbed her hands over the suitcase, but just as she peeled off the key to unlock it, her daddy put his hand on her shoulder and said, "Not now, Lilah. Only the magician should see what makes up her tool kit."

"He's right for a change," Nana Belle said. "The kit is for your eyes only. Ultimate secrecy is imperative."

Lilah looked at Ruthie and then at Jill. "Imperative" sounded important. They never kept secrets from each other. She didn't know if she could keep this one.

"It's okay, Girlfriend," Ruthie said. "Jilly and I can help you when you want it."

"We'll be your PR," said Jilly.

Lilah knew all about PR. PR stood for Public Relations, and that's what her mother did at the sugar company. It meant getting other people to notice you and like you.

"Right," said Ruthie. "We can make posters and get an interview on your daddy's radio show to get the word out."

"Wait'll the kids see you at Showtime," said Jilly. She rubbed her hands together in excitement.

"Hold it a minute," said Lilah. "You're rushing me. My daddy would say that you're putting the cart before the horse. I don't even have an act yet. First of all I have to get in here and learn these tricks, and rehearse them. And I guess I'm going to have to do it alone." She hadn't thought of that before.

"One more thing," Polly said. She stood behind Lilah and wrapped a beautiful black satin cape around Lilah's shoulders. "You can't be a true magician without a proper cape."

Lilah looked up at her smiling mother and didn't feel so anxious. The cape was heavy and deliciously smooth, the inside lined with ruby red silk. Across the back, 'Shagundula' was embroidered in red satin thread. Two big buttons held the cape closed at the neck and a stand-up collar framed Lilah's happy face. She was almost a magician.

CHAPTER SIX

The Magician's Apprentice

After school, the next day, Lilah sat on the fluffy white rug in the middle of her bedroom. All the pieces of her kit surrounded her. The bedroom door was closed, and on the outside of the door was a sign that read, KEEP OUT—MAGICIAN AT WORK.

Lilah had taken a peek at the magic kit the night before, but the cups and ropes and little boxes were a mystery. Now, the magic kit instructions, which came in a special booklet, lay before her with all of the secrets. Lilah tried reading, but the tiny print was so full of big words that she couldn't understand what she was supposed to do. Her shoulder muscles tensed up and she twisted in frustration. *Magic just shouldn't be this hard*, she thought.

Poking out from under some scarves was the magic wand, black with a white tip. Lilah picked it up. It felt light in her hand, so she waved it a few times. Nothing happened. She pointed the wand at Buster, who lay under the bed.

"Abracadabra," she said.

Nothing.

She waved the wand at the closed curtains. "Alacazam."

Nothing.

"Shazam!" She shouted this time, waving it at Buster.

Buster pounced into the pile of scarves and began batting them around.

Well, she thought, *so much for magic. I guess I'm going to have to use my brains and my fantabulous showmanship after all. But I don't know what to do with this stuff.*

There was a soft knock on the door.

"Madam Shagundula?"

"Yes?" she said. She knew it was her daddy.

"Are you ready to show us a little of your magic?"

"Not yet, Daddy," she said. "Maybe later."

"Just one little trick?"

"No!"

"You know," Darius said. "Most magicians have an apprentice."

"What's that?"

"It's a magician's helper."

Silence.

"Someone that helps the magician with the illusions, but is sworn to secrecy."

"Yeah?" *Hmm*, thought Lilah. *I could use a helper.* "Any suggestions?" she asked.

CHAPTER SEVEN

Dress Rehearsal

It had been two weeks since Lilah had invited her daddy into her room to help her with her magic. Darius, the magician's apprentice, was especially good at figuring out all of the directions to the tricks, or "illusions." That's what they were really called.

Shagundula stood before her mama's mirror in her magician's costume. Today she and her daddy were going to do a dress rehearsal in front of the Chicks,

Bongo and Jonny-cake. Darius, the apprentice, came in and stood next to her. He wore his tuxedo outfit without the coat so that he looked less important than Shagundula.

They could hear the Chicks laughing over their martinis while they waited for their show. Lilah tiptoed into the hall and peeked around the corner to see Bongo and Jonny-cake warming their audience with a drum and cat act. Bongo beat on the drums he was named for, and Jonny-cake danced Buster around in time with the beat.

Lilah could tell that Buster wasn't going to put up with it much longer, so she strode, clapping, into center stage of the living room, and announced, "Let's give a hand to these talented young entertainers."

The Chicks applauded and the boys took their bows, while Buster dug his claws into Jonny-cake's leg. At that point, it was hard to tell who was howling the most.

As Lilah's mama took Jonny-cake off to the bathroom, Lilah ducked back into the hall and motioned to her apprentice. "Okay Daddy, break a leg," she whispered. That meant "good luck" in theater talk.

Darius entered center stage with a TV tray covered in a black cloth. He placed it and announced, "Ladies and Gentlemen, I am proud to present the one, the only, Madam Shagundula the Magician!"

Lilah strode out onto the stage, her cape flying behind her. The Chicks sat on the couch and her mama sat in the big wing chair with both boys in her lap. Buster was nowhere in sight.

"Welcome one and all," Lilah said. "Tonight you will marvel at my command over the mystical powers of the universe." She smiled confidently. She had created and practiced that line many times and was quite proud of it.

She continued. "Will my apprentice, Darius, please bring two glasses of water?" . . . and so it went. Her first two illusions; the disappearing water and the magic handkerchief, went quite smoothly. And now she was ready for her next illusion—The Magic Clock.

Lilah held up a small cardboard clock. "As you can plainly see, I have a clock with the dials set at the correct time. When I turn my back, I would like one of you to change the hands and then put the clock out of my sight." She placed it on the TV tray, turned her back and heard some scuffling around and whispering.

"Okay" said Bongo. "We're ready."

"We'll get back to that in a minute," Lilah said. She went on with a simple card trick and then got back to the clock. "Now, I will turn my back again while you change the hands on the clock back to the correct time."

Again, some scuffling and whispering, and when she turned around Bongo presented her with the clock. "At this point," Lilah said. "We will have a short break, after which I will tell you what time you had changed the clock to."

Polly went to the kitchen for more refreshments and Lilah went into the coat closet. She needed it pitch dark to see the glow-in-the-dark lines, left by the clock hands so she'd know where they had been. It was really hard to see and so she waited, thinking that the lines just hadn't shown up yet. She felt like she'd been in the closet for quite a long time, but she still couldn't see the lines. Something had gone wrong.

CHAPTER EIGHT

Rock Around the Clock

Lilah, still in the closet, could hear Darius's voice and the Chicks laughing quite loudly. It didn't sound like she needed to rush back. She looked at the clock again, but it hadn't changed. *The trick wasn't working. What to do?*

Lilah heard a soft knock on the closet door, and then a whisper, "Delilah, it's Mama. Do you need any help?"

"No," she said. "I'm fine."

"Is the magic clock working?"

"Not yet." Lilah's voice sounded shaky and scared.

"Maybe it's broken. I don't want you to lose your audience. Why don't you come out and make a joke about the magic clock. Say that it magically flew away."

Lilah thought about that. *Not a bad idea.* The clock still wasn't giving her a clue about the set time.

"Okay Mama. You go sit down now and act like you never talked to me."

"Okay Lilah. But hurry."

Well, the show must go on. That's what her daddy always said. Lilah slipped the clock into her pocket and walked back out into the living room. Darius was standing at center stage, wearing his tuxedo coat . . . and he was performing one of Lilah's illusions—the rice bowls. It was one of the tricks that she was going to do.

She felt a blush crawl up her neck. She suddenly felt small and embarrassed . . . and angry with her daddy. *How dare he steal one of my tricks!*

She looked at the Chicks and the twins. They were laughing and shrieking with amazement.

"How did he do that?" asked the Chick on the couch.

"He's awesome!" said Jonny-cake.

"I'm back," said Lilah, dramatically whipping her cape back, "and I have to tell you about the magic clock."

Everybody got very quiet and looked at Lilah. Now she wished that she hadn't interrupted.

She took a deep breath and said, "The reason I've been gone so long is because the magic clock flew out of my hand. Little wings sprouted and it flew away. I chased it for a little while but finally gave up, knowing that you were all waiting for me." They all laughed and clapped while she glared at her father.

"Good save," her Daddy whispered. Then he spoke loudly, so that the audience could hear, "Shagundula, please bring me the magic coin box."

Lilah was so stunned that she looked into her kit, found the magic coin box, and took it to her father. She hadn't worked with that one yet. She tried to gain control of the audience. After all, it was her act.

Holding the painted box up to the audience, she said, in her best stage voice, "As you can plainly see, I am handing my apprentice, Darius, a magic coin box."

Darius took the box and proceeded to do the trick where he kept pulling coins out, letting Bongo and Lisa Chick examine the empty box, and then pulled more coins out of it. Lilah had to admit, he was a very good magician—maybe better than Shagundula. She was getting a little stomach-ache and wanted the act to end.

"Thank you Ladies and Gentlemen for coming to our magic show," said Lilah. "We have enjoyed entertaining you and wish you a good evening."

Applause.

With that she gave a deep bow and then put her hand out towards Darius. "And let's hear it for my apprentice, Darius Dill."

More applause.

She studied her daddy. He looked surprised that the show had ended so soon, but he took a bow.

"To Shagundula!" he said, with his arm outstretched to Lilah.

But it was too late. The applause had ended. The Chicks were already diving into the chips and dip while the twins practiced their new tumbling stunts.

Lilah gathered up her tricks and took them to her room where she could return them to their kit in an orderly way. She wanted to be alone. She felt like she was going to cry and she didn't want anybody to see. She flung herself down on her bed, hugging her stuffed dog.

Suddenly Mama was there, lightly stroking her back. "There, there," she said. "You did a great job for your first show. What's one little trick?"

It really wasn't the magic clock that had upset Lilah the most, but she didn't want to admit that to her mother. Her father had stolen her act!

Somehow, things had gotten switched and she had become the sorcerer's apprentice instead of the sorcerer. She felt like she had lost her magical powers. Magic was going to take a lot more practice than she thought.

CHAPTER NINE

Best Friends

Jilly, Lilah and Ruthie sat on the bench at the edge of the school playground, eating their lunches. It had been two weeks since the dress rehearsal and Lilah had finally confided in her two best friends.

"Just talk to your daddy," Jilly said. "Tell him that it's your act and that he can't steal your tricks."

"I can't do that," said Lilah. She looked down at her silver bracelet and rubbed the silver hat.

Ruthie spoke with her mouth full of apple. "No, I couldn't say that to my father. He'd yell at me and say that he never gets any respect and would probably send me to my room."

Lilah shook her head. "It's not that. It's just that. . ." She stopped.

"It's what?" demanded Jilly.

"It's just that his feelings would be hurt. I know that he was only trying to help me, and I think he just got carried away. If there's an audience, well . . ."

Lilah slumped, knowing that her daddy just couldn't help himself in front of an audience. He just had to perform. *Nana Belle is that way too*, she thought.

"So, time to try it again," said Jilly. "This time Ruthie and I can be your apprentices."

"Right," said Ruthie.

"But when and where?" asked Lilah.

Ruthie wiped her mouth with her napkin. "There's going to be a Showtime Talent Night in the school auditorium, and we can do the act then."

Lilah looked down at her swinging feet, thinking about Showtime. It was a really big deal. Jilly balled up her empty lunch bag and tossed it into the garbage can that sat against the fence. "Two points for that perfect throw. You know we don't have much time to get ready. Auditions are next week."

"You guys are the best," said Lilah. "Thanks for helping. I'm getting that happy feeling again."

Jilly and Ruthie spoke together. "That's what friends are for."

Lilah put an arm around each of them, feeling stronger. This was starting to sound like a good idea. It would take a lot of practice for Ruthie and Jilly to learn their parts, and she would have to practice so that the audience would be truly amazed at her magic skills. A little bud of hope began blossoming in Lilah's heart. But first she had to fire her daddy.

CHAPTER TEN

Roll Out the Barrel

It was 3 o'clock when Lilah walked up the driveway to her house and she could hear piano music coming out of every open window. That could only mean one thing—Nana Belle.

"Roll out the barrel, we'll have a barrel of fun," Nana sang out.

Lilah opened the door and jumped into the room. "Fun, fun, fun," she sang. She knew that Nana must have been watching for her because this was one of her favorite songs.

Nana continued singing as she banged on the piano keys, "Roll out the barrel, we've got the blues on the run."

"Run, run, run."

Together, they sang, "Zing, boom, tar-errel, sing out a song of good cheer. Now's the time to roll the barrel, for the gang's all here." That last line was sung so loudly and with such good cheer that they both held onto the last note for eight counts.

Lilah threw her books on the floor and wrapped her arms around Nana Belle's shoulders. "Nana Belle, I've missed you so much," she said.

Nana Belle gave her a big kiss on the cheek and she could feel the tangerine lipstick drying on her skin. "I wanted to surprise you and I guess I did."

Lilah looked around and saw no sign of her father. "Where's Daddy?" she asked.

"Oh he had to cover for someone else at the radio station. Looks like he's going to be taking double shifts for a couple of weeks. Your mom thought that it might be a good time for me to come and stay for awhile."

Lilah liked that idea, but she wondered when she'd get a chance to talk to her daddy. "Nana," she asked, "Do you think that it would be okay to have Jilly and Ruthie over tomorrow—after school, I mean? I want them to help me with my magic."

Nana Belle spun around on the piano stool and faced Lilah. "Well, of course Lilah, but I thought that your father was helping with the magic."

"Well . . . he was . . . and, well, now he's going to be too busy so I'll need to train some new apprentices."

Nana Belle smoothed Lilah's hair back, looked into her eyes, and said, "Shagundula, you are the best one to decide about that. Let's give Ruthie and Jilly's parents a phone call."

Jonny-cake and Bongo came running into the family room. "Nana, Nana, Pepper isn't in his cage and we've looked everywhere!"

Lilah looked around with a queasy feeling in her stomach. All of the windows were open. "Did you leave the cage door open?" she asked, already knowing the answer.

"Yes," said Bongo. "He likes to throw silverware off the table."

Jonny-cake added, "He peeks over the edge and watches the spoons hit the floor."

Lilah looked at the table and saw no Sergeant Pepper—just a lot of spoons on the floor. "Oh no, what if he flew outside?" she cried.

"Now now," said Nana. "You keep looking inside and I'll look outside. By the way, where's Buster?"

The twins looked at each other with big eyes. They turned and ran through the house looking for Buster and Pepper. Lilah, wiping her own eyes, could hear them calling for the bird and the cat as they ran from room to room. She wasn't worried about Buster, she just hoped he wasn't with Pepper.

A frantic peeping sound came from the kitchen. Lilah ran into the kitchen and saw something that made her very happy. A dirty drinking glass, lined with orange pulp, sat by the sink. Inside the glass was a trapped parakeet standing on his head, wings pinned to his side. "Peep, peep, squawk, peep squawk!" Sergeant Pepper sounded very angry and scared.

"You silly bird," Lilah laughed, much relieved. "That's what you get for being so greedy." She lifted the glass and started to slide him out when she had an idea. She took the trapped parakeet into her bedroom.

Several minutes later, Madam Shagundula walked back into the family room wearing her cape and holding her wand. Nana and the twins were all sitting on the couch. The twins were crying and Nana was consoling them. She looked up to see Shagundula's entrance. "Lilah," she said. "Now is not a good time to practice your magic act."

Shagundula looked around, the windows were all closed. "On the contrary," she said. "It's the perfect time." She held out her black top hat. "As you can plainly see, this is merely an empty hat." She showed the hat to Nana Belle and the twins, who were watching closely.

"Not now, Shagundula," Nana said, more firmly this time.

Lilah ignored her. "But, let's see if the Great Madam Shagundula can make some magic." Lilah waved her wand over the hat. " Allah kazam, allah kazepper, watch while I show you the great Sergeant Pepper."

She shook the hat and held it to the

side. Pepper flew out and landed right on top of Nana Belle's head where he laid a great big parakeet poop. Nana Belle gave out a little scream.

"Pepper!" Bongo screamed. "It's Sergeant Pepper. Oh Lilah, you are a magician!"

Nana Belle put her finger under the parakeet to make a little perch. Pepper jumped onto her finger and Nana headed off to the cage. "Now, she said, "nobody open the cage door while Nana washes her hair. And Madam Shagundula, that was a lovely illusion. Well done."

Lilah went off to her room feeling like the magnificent magician that she was. *Tomorrow I'll start training my apprentices,* she thought, *but I still have to fire my daddy.*

CHAPTER ELEVEN

Teamwork

Two days later, Jilly, Ruthie and Lilah sat on the fluffy white rug in Lilah's bedroom. The sign on the door read; KEEP OUT, MAGIC AT WORK. The pink ballerina clock, next to Lilah's bed, read three-thirty.

Ruthie tied a blue scarf around her arm as she said, "I think that three tricks are enough, so lets practice how we're going to do them."

"First of all," said Lilah, "you're going to have to take off all of those scarves if you're going to be pulling them out of your pocket."

"Who me?" asked Ruthie.

"Yes you," said Jilly. "Who else has a million scarves hanging off of their limbs?"

"Limbs? Do you think I'm a tree?" Ruthie put her arms up in a tree pose. "But I didn't know that I was going to have to perform."

Lilah placed the magic rice bowls on the bed. "You're just going to do a little warm-up, as I introduce you, and then I'll hit them with the biggies."

"I know that I'm going to take Cornball's place doing the music," said Jilly, putting her hands on her hips. "But I don't know when to play what. And I guess I'm going to have to learn how to work the stereo."

"No problem," said Lilah as she placed the magic coin box on her bed. "I'll show you how to do all that stuff, and we can practice your cues tomorrow." She walked over to her closet and started digging through her big pink trunk. "Ah, here it is." She pulled out some black tights and leotards and threw them to Ruthie. "Here's your costume, Ruthie."

Ruthie held the leotard up in front of her. "Wait a minute, girlfriend. Is that all I'm going to wear? It looks a little skimpy to me . . . and plain."

Lilah still digging, said, "Just hold on, I've got a red cummerbund in here somewhere."

Ruthie walked over to the closet and peered in. "What's a crumber bun?" she asked.

Jilly giggled. "Not a crumber, it's a cummerbund—like a wide sashy thing that men wear around their middle. My daddy has a white one."

"Why would I wear something that men wear around their middle?" Ruthie sounded annoyed.

"Well, my daddy and I wore them with our tuxedos," Lilah said, her head deep into the pink trunk. "Black ones and . . . oh finally. Here it is." She pulled out a bright red satin cummerbund.

"Boy is that red!" Ruthie said. "I like it!"

"And here's a little red hat to match." Lilah threw it over her shoulder and Ruthie caught it. "Oh, and a red bowtie with sequins. Perfect."

"What about me?" asked Jilly, eyes in a squint. "Don't I get a costume? I could

wear a Hawaiian shirt like Cornball."

"No Hawaiian shirts," said Lilah. "The backstage techies usually wear all black, and quiet shoes, so they can sneak around without anyone noticing—like burglars. Here's some black ballet shoes."

"Oh goody," said Jilly, "I'll dress like a burglar. Can I borrow that black cat mask on your dresser?"

"Sure," said Lilah. "It was waiting for you. Now, let's get to work." *This is so much fun,* she thought. *We make a great team.*

~

At five o'clock there was a knock on the door, and Nana Belle's voice said, "May I come in?"

"Come on in, Nana," said Lilah. "We're all done and we're just visiting."

The three girls were all lying on their backs, across Lilah's bed, so that when Nana walked in Lilah could see Nana's upside down mouth, much bigger and floppier than her mama's. Jilly had been talking about what it would be like to go around upside down for a whole day. The floor would be the ceiling and the ceiling the floor. It would be a magical upside-down world.

"Jilly's mom is here to take you two home," Nana said. "It's almost dinner time." Ruthie and Jilly jumped up and collected their things. Ruthie carefully folded the new costumes for herself and for Jilly.

"Oh, already?" said Lilah, as her head slid to the rug. "I wish you could stay."

"Didn't you get enough practice in, sweetie?' asked Nana.

"Oh yes, we got a lot done. But we still need to practice some more. Can they come again tomorrow?"

"It's fine with me, as long as you get your homework done, but they'll have to ask their folks you know."

Lilah, Nana and the twins stood on the front porch and waved good-bye just as Lilah's father drove into the driveway. *Uh-oh*, thought Lilah, *there's still some unfinished business.*

CHAPTER TWELVE

Hula Noodles

Lilah's mama arrived home from work just in time to sit down to Nana Belle's chicken stroganoff. Lilah usually loved chicken stroganoff, but on this night, with her daddy on her mind, the noodles felt like they were doing a hula dance in her stomach.

Mama decided to move the dinner to the lanai, being it was such nice weather. Usually, Lilah enjoyed eating dinner out in the fresh air with her whole family, but she couldn't enjoy it as much because her mind was working hard at coming up with the right words. How was she going to tell her daddy that he was no longer her apprentice? Out of the blue, he beat her to it.

"Lilah," said Daddy, "Have you heard about Showtime Talent Night coming up at your school?" He said this in a casual way that made it seem like it wasn't very important. Or maybe he sounded that way because he was using his napkin to clean up Bongo's spilled milk. Lilah wasn't sure.

"Mhmm," said Lilah. She tried to sound casual too, like it wasn't something she'd thought a lot about.

"Your principal came down to the station and made an announcement about it.

The auditions are soon. Are you planning to do your magic act?"

"Mhmm." Lilah said this as quietly as possible, moving her noodles around the plate.

"Well we don't have much time, Madam Shagundula," he said, rubbing his hands together. "We better start practicing." Her daddy's eyes had happy crinkles at the corners as he gave her a little poke.

Lilah noticed that he said "we" without even asking her if he could be in it.

Lilah's mama jumped in. "Are they allowing parents to be in it this year?" she asked. She sounded casual too.

"Yes," said Darius. "I asked just to make sure. You do want me to be your apprentice, don't you?"

All through this conversation Nana Belle had been unusually quiet. Lilah looked to her for help but Nana silently started to help Mama remove the dirty dishes. She was on her own this time.

Speaking softly, she said. "I know how hard you've been working at the radio station and so I asked Ruthie and Jilly to help me."

"Oh, okay, that makes sense," her daddy said. His eyes stopped the happy crinkling. He was quiet for awhile, so was Lilah, and so was everybody else. Lilah pretended to be studying the way her button was sewed on to her blouse. She didn't want to hurt her father, and she thought that he sounded very hurt. She knew that she was supposed to say something more, but she couldn't think of what to say.

Nana Belle broke the silence. "The girls have been practicing and work together so well. They're a great team."

"Oh, well, that's good," he said. He looked down at his plate. Then he smiled at Lilah and said, "Well, if you need any help . . ."

It was quiet again. Lilah could hear the water in the kitchen sink go on and off as her mama rinsed the plates. She peeked up at her father and his face looked red. It didn't feel good— to upset her daddy.

After dinner, Daddy helped the twins take out the garbage and then they stayed out to play bounce and catch, which left the ladies in the kitchen.

"Mama," asked Lilah, "do you think that Daddy is mad at me?"

"Oh no, Delilah, I think that he just got

his nose pushed out of shape."

Lilah pictured her daddy's nose changing into different shapes—long and skinny, big and bulbous, blobbing over to one side. She liked her daddy's nose just the way it was.

Just then the phone rang. Nana Belle answered it and said, "Polly, it's for you." It was Jilly's mom, making arrangements for practice the next day. Ruthie's mom had called earlier.

Well, thought Lilah, *here we go. I've fired my daddy and, except for Jilly and Ruthie, I'm on my own.*

CHAPTER THIRTEEN

The Audition

Jilly, Ruthie and Lilah sat on the cold metal folding chairs in the Sugar City School's auditorium. Lilah sniffed at the left over odors of cafeteria lunch and afternoon P.E., which blended to create that familiar auditorium smell.

She felt ready for the audition. They had practiced all week and were now waiting for their turn. *We really look splendid in our costumes. We'll look even better with our make-up.*

Nevertheless, Lilah couldn't stop fidgeting. She studied her friends. Ruthie drummed her hands on her knees and Jilly, squinting as usual, looked like she was deep into her comic book. *Yep, they were ready too.*

Mrs. Krouch, the teacher who was director of the show, looked down at her clip board and called out, "Katrina Petrov, come to the stage. You're on." Mrs. Krouch then blew her nose so loudly that it sounded like a goose honking.

Katrina attended Lilah's ballet class and always acted like she thought she was hot stuff. Lilah didn't know her all that well, so she hadn't invited her to her birthday party, but now she smiled at Katrina.

Katrina stood up and brushed right past Lilah without so much as a nod. Her scratchy white tutu brushed against Jilly's hand, causing Jilly to drop her comic book.

"Hey," said Jilly.

No apologies from Katrina. *That's not her style*, thought Lilah.

Katrina carried a CD with her and handed it to Mrs. Krouch on the way to the stage. Mrs. Krouch slipped the CD into the player.

"Please introduce yourself and your act," said Mrs. Krouch, as she had with every act before Katrina.

Katrina stood very tall and announced, "I am Katrina Petrov and will perform The Dying Swan from Swan Lake."

"This I gotta see," Ruthie whispered, fanning herself with a paper fan she'd just made.

Katrina raised her hands to fifth position and nodded her head to Mrs. Krouch. "You may begin the music."

Mrs. Krouch pressed the play button and Katrina started to dance. She had a heavy step, and the audience could hear the clomping sounds of large ballerina feet hitting the floorboards as Katrina attempted a turning leap called a *tour jete.*

The dying part was slow, with much arm waving and looks of pain on the dying swan's face. Lilah felt relief when it ended, and she let out a "whoosh" of air. It had been such torture to watch, that her eyes ached.

Ruthie jabbed Lilah in the ribs. "That was one klutzy swan, Girlfriend."

Lilah tried to hold her giggle in, but a snort slipped out.

"No kiddin'," piped Jilly. Her comic book forgotten, she laughed out loud.

Mrs. Krouch glared at the girls, her enormous chest puffed up in anger. "I must remind you that I will not tolerate any disrespect from the audience."

Three heads looked down and got very quiet.

Two more acts took their turns—four fifth-grade boys doing a silly skit and then a tall skinny boy who performed the same piano solo every year. That made fourteen auditions so far.

"Delilah Dilitis, Ruth Taylor and Jillian Frost, please come to the stage.

"Here goes," whispered Lilah. "Break a leg."

The three girls walked up to the stage, Jilly slipping behind the curtain wings with her sound equipment.

"Do you have a CD for me?" asked Mrs. Krouch. She leaned forward and Lilah could see a tissue stuffed into the neck of her blouse.

"Oh no," said Lilah. "I travel with my own sound techie—Jilly Frost."

Jilly, cat mask in place, peeked out from behind the curtain and wiggled her fingers in a little wave. Ruthie was busy setting up the TV tray and the magic props.

"Please introduce yourselves and your act," said Mrs. Krouch. She sounded tired and a little bit grouchy. She made two more nose blows. *Honk. Honk.*

"My name is Lilah Dill and I, as Madam Shagundula, will perform an amazing, a most mystifying, an utterly . . . "

"Lilah, just introduce your act," interrupted Mrs. Krouch. "*Honk*."

"That's what I was doing. Now where was I? Oh yeah, an utterly . . ."

"Delilah!" Mrs. Krouch barked. "Cut to the chase."

Lilah was confused. "The chase?"

"*Honk. Honk. Honk.* Yes, the act. Skip most of your introduction please. I don't have all day. The other girls need to introduce themselves too." She tucked her tissue back into her dress.

"I was going to introduce my apprentice and my techie at the end of the act," said Lilah.

Jilly peeked out again, waved again and said, "Hi, I'm Jilly."

Ruthie looked up from the TV tray. "Oh, and I'm Ruthie. Ruthie Taylor."

Jilly peeked out again. "Frost! Jilly Frost!" she yelled.

Lilah started again. "I, Madam Shagundula, welcome you to observe unbelievable magic tricks and acts of . . ."

"All right already," shouted Mrs. Krouch as she gathered up her papers. "*Honk.* That's good enough."

She looked up at the clock on the back wall. "You're finished. We've run out of time and I think I'm catching a cold. I'll see you Friday night. Be here at six-thirty sharp. *Honk. Honk.*" She turned and strode toward the back of the auditorium.

"But you haven't even seen our illusions," Lilah protested.

Mrs. Krouch opened the door and yelled over her shoulder, "Fold up your chairs and put them away before leaving.

Don't forget—six-thirty—Friday night. And with one final *"Honk,"* the door slammed and she was gone.

Jilly peeked out from behind the curtain one more time. "Well, that went well," she said.

CHAPTER 14

Best Laid Plans

Lilah threw the bed sheets back and looked at her ballerina clock. Friday. Six-thirty, am. *Tonight's the night*, she thought, feeling a little quiver of excitement in her belly. *Am I really ready?*

Buster sauntered into the bedroom to greet her, like he did every morning, rubbing up against her and winding in and out of the space between her ankles. Lilah bent over and picked him up, burying her face in his thick fur. "Good morning,

Kitty," she said.

"Purrrrr," said Buster.

"How do you always know the exact moment that I wake up?"

Buster answered by pushing his nose into Lilah's cheek.

"Come and get it! Chow time! Breakfast is on the plank," Darius yelled. He was pretending that he was running a chuck wagon. "Giddyap on down here before it gets cold, buckaroos."

Lilah giggled. He came up with the goofiest ideas.

"I'm a-comin' Pa," she yelled back, putting Buster on the floor. She threw on her bathrobe and headed towards the kitchen. "I hope that you wrastled me up a big ol' breakfast steak."

Lilah collided with the twins in the

hallway as they all rushed to be the first to get to the kitchen. Both twins were dressed in red and blue overalls and cowboy boots. Somebody must have been up early to dress them.

Lilah's daddy stood at the stove in his sweats, stirring oatmeal, while her mama sat at the breakfast bar sipping a cup of coffee and reading the newspaper. She looked all dressed for work and ready to go.

"Mornin' little dogies," Daddy said.

"We're not doggies?" said Bongo. "We're cowboys!"

"Yeah!" said Jonny-cake. "Cowboys!"

Polly put down the paper, looking them up and down. "Good morning, Sweet Peas. Nice duds."

"Yep," Bongo said, holding one boot in the air. "Cowboy duds!"

"Yes, I see that," said Polly, but you're going to have to eat wiki wiki 'cause I'm taking you to school and childcare on my way to the hospital. Nana needs some tests."

"Tests?" asked Lilah. "Is she okay?"

"Oh yes, she's fine. The doctor wanted to do a check up. I just hope that she feels well enough to attend Showtime."

Lilah didn't like the sound of that. She really wanted Nana to see how well all of the practicing had turned out.

All three kids climbed onto the bar stools to eat their breakfast. Lilah, still thinking about Nana Belle, was caught by surprise with what her father had to say.

"Polly, I hope that you can get everyone to Showtime tonight. I won't be able to go because they're having me cover for Radio Ron."

Lilah couldn't believe her ears. "You mean you're not going to see my magic act?" she asked. Her chin started to tremble, and then a sudden thought popped into her head—*maybe he doesn't want to see my show.* For the first time, Lilah realized how important it was for her daddy to see her starring in her own magic act. She wanted to surprise him and make him proud. Holding back the tears as best she could, she looked down at the lumpy oatmeal in her breakfast bowl.

"I'm sorry kiddo. I have to work. I'll try to get there, but if I can't, your mom can take a lot of pictures, or maybe a video. Can't you, Polly?"

"What?" asked Mama. Her voice sounded sharp and strained. "Darius, you just need to tell the station that your daughter is performing at a school event and you have to be there. Sure I can take pictures but it's not the same."

"I just don't think that's gonna fly," he said, wiping his hands on a dishtowel.

"Sergeant Pepper can fly," said Jonny-cake. The parakeet peeped from his cage in agreement.

"What about Wolfman? He owes you a couple of favors," said Mama.

Bongo let out a wolf howl.

Daddy paused for a moment while he scooped some oatmeal into Bongo's bowl. "We'll see. I'll try to get a hold of him this morning and ask." His eyes darted to Lilah then back to the bowl.

Lilah couldn't stop thinking that there was more to it. *Maybe Daddy's mad at me because he's not in it,* she thought. She looked at him, closely. *Maybe his nose is still pushed out of place.*

She squinted her eyes shut and tried to read his mind, but her magic skills weren't that good.

~

Later that day, Lilah stood behind Jilly in line at the four square game.

"I think Ruthie went home, sick," said Jilly. "Her mom came to school and picked her up."

Lilah's heart sunk into her stomach. "Oh no. What about our act? I was totally depending on her. We rehearsed it all those times . . . we don't even know where she put the TV tray and all the rest of my magic kit!"

"Maybe she'll feel better by tonight," said Jilly, eyes on the game.

"That's a big maybe. What'll we do if she's not?"

"Let's worry about that later," said Jilly. She stepped into an open square. "Don't talk to me now." She whacked at the bouncing ball with both hands. "I have to concentrate on four square."

Doesn't anybody care? thought Lilah. The ball rolled across the playground and Lilah didn't even bother to chase it. Her thoughts were very blue. *Everything is going wrong—first Nana, then Daddy and now Ruthie. What else could happen?*

CHAPTER FIFTEEN

The Bells are Ringing

The phone rang and Lilah jumped up from the table, hoping that it was Ruthie's mother saying that she'd be at the auditorium in time for the show. Polly beat her to the phone, but Lilah leaned in to her mama, listening to Polly's end of the conversation.

"Yes. Oh, hello. Yes, yes, I see. Oh, that's too bad."

That didn't sound good. Lilah looked at the clock above the door. Five thirty. Time to put her tuxedo and make-up on.

Her mama, still on the phone, was quiet, listening to the other person talk. She motioned to Lilah to sit down.

"Is it Ruthie's mom?" Lilah whispered in her best stage whisper.

Her mama nodded up and down.

"What's she sayin'?" asked Lilah.

Polly put her hand up for quiet.

"Are they going to make it?"

"Okay, yes. Well, thanks for calling. Yes, I'll be sure to tell Lilah. Yes. Bye bye."

It turned out that Ruthie had left school because of a dental appointment in the city. On their way home, there had been an accident and Ruthie and her mom were still stuck in traffic.

"So," Polly said, "Mrs. Taylor told me that they'd do their best to get to the auditorium in time for your act. She wants you to ask Mrs. Krouch if you can go last. That'll give them a little more time."

Lilah let that sink in. "Mama, you need to call her back and ask her where she put my magic kit," she said, pushing her plate away.

"She said that it was in the Green Room cupboard, next to the sink. No need to worry, Delilah, I'm sure that Ruthie will make it in time. For now, finish up your dinner. I don't want you going with an empty stomach."

Lilah, the twins and Polly, sat back down to their light supper of tuna sandwiches. Lilah wasn't at all hungry, again. Daddy was still at work and they hadn't heard from him. She tried not to think about that. She tried to picture happy things—like rabbits hopping out of hats and colored scarves turning into a rainbow.

The phone rang again. Polly jumped up and answered it. "Oh, hi Mom. You do? Are you sure? Okay, I'll be sure to tell Lilah. We'll pick you up in a half hour. Bye bye."

"Hurray," shouted Lilah. "Nana Belle's coming! She is, isn't she?"

Polly laughed. "Yes, that was your Nana. She's feeling good and said that she wouldn't miss your show if she had to crawl there on all fours."

"She's so dramatic," said Lilah, rolling her eyes. But then she couldn't stop herself. She jumped up, put her hands in the air, and did a dramatic little happy dance, singing, "Nana's comin', Nana's comin'!"

Bongo and Jonny-cake jumped up and joined in the happy dance.

Mama laughed. "Hurray, everything's working out. Let's get your make-up on and then gather up your things, 'cause we need to get moving. Jilly's mom said that she'd meet up with us at the school. Boys, wash your hands and faces."

CHAPTER SIXTEEN

The Green Room

Lilah and Jilly ran up to the back door of the auditorium, hoping that nobody would see them.

"It's best to surprise the audience," Lilah told Jilly. "If they see you in your costume beforehand, it'll ruin the surprise."

Jilly opened the door and they stepped into the behind-the-stage Green Room. Most of the other acts were already there. Some kids sat on folding chairs, some were at the mirrors, putting their make-up on. The silly skit boys were chasing each other around the room. Lilah shook her head in a disapproving manner.

Mrs. Krouch, puffed up with importance and perspiring heavily, rushed in one door, and then out of the other door.

"Why do they call this the Green Room," asked Jilly. "It looks beige to me."

"All of the rooms behind stages are called "Green Rooms." The color doesn't matter," said Lilah. She took the freshly ironed cape off of the hanger that her mama had handed to her.

"Well, it should matter. I'll be calling this the Beige Room from now on. It's more honest."

The biggest thing on Lilah's mind was to get to Mrs. Krouch to see if they could be the last act in the show.

"You watch for Ruthie," she said to Jilly, as she buttoned on her cape, "and I'll try to get to Mrs. Krouch."

Jilly pointed to the TV tray folded up and leaning against the wall. "Phew!" she said. "There's the tray. I'll get the kit out of the cupboard while you're doing that."

Mrs. Krouch strutted around, Lilah on her tail, begging her to let them be the last act. "Please Mrs. Krouch," she said. "Ruthie can't help it and she really needs to be there or my act will be a flop!"

At last Mrs. Krouch gave up, grumbling. "Okay, okay, you're last, just stop following me around."

That calmed Lilah's nerves a little, until Jilly found her and said, "I can't find your magic kit anywhere! I've looked in every cupboard!"

"I knew that I should have taken it home," Lilah cried. "Somebody must have stolen my magic tricks."

CHAPTER SEVENTEEN

Hide and Seek

Katrina, the ballet dancer, was stretching her right leg by resting her large foot on the counter of the sink. "I think that I saw your magic box in the audio-visual closet," she said, looking in the mirror. "Is that what you're looking for?"

"I'm on it," said Jilly and she started to run out of the room. She turned around and asked, "What audio-visual closet?"

"Behind the curtains," said Katrina, rolling her eyes. "Stage right."

"Right," said Jilly. This time both Jilly and Lilah headed to the back of the stage.

Together, they crept behind the back curtains, stepping in and around old scenery until they could get to the closet. They could hear the silly boys doing their skit, so they knew they had to be as quiet as cats and at the same time not ruffle the curtains.

Finally they arrived at the closet. Just when Lilah opened the door, something huge loomed over her. She screamed and the silly skit got dead quiet. There was some nervous laughter from the audience.

Mrs. Krouch was the something huge and looming. She whispered, "What do you think you're doing back here!"

They listened for the silly skit to continue, and then Jilly whispered, "We're getting the magic kit."

Mrs. Krouch shined a flashlight into the closet. An old record player and a blanket filled up the corner, no magic kit to be seen. Lilah's stomach twisted.

Jilly leaned past her and picked up the blanket. There sat the beautiful blue box with the moons and stars, the prettiest sight that Lilah could remember since she'd first seen it on her birthday.

"If that's it then hurry up and take it back to the Green Room," whispered Mrs. Krouch. She dabbed her forehead with a wadded-up tissue. "And don't move the curtains!"

They tip-toed back to the Green Room, Lilah carrying the magic kit.

Once they got there she opened it, took out the props she'd need, and took some time checking them out and putting them on the covered TV tray.

"There," Lilah murmured. "Now all we need is Ruthie."

The silly skit boys came back into the room and Mrs. Krouch signaled to Katrina to go back stage. Lilah couldn't calm herself down. She paced back and forth, back and forth, until she caught her reflection in the mirror. The girl in the mirror wasn't Shagundulah at all. She looked like some scared little girl in a magician's costume. Lilah stopped her pacing, faced the mirror and said, "I am Shagundula the Magician. Woman of Mystery and Illusion."

"Yes you are," said Jilly, looking up from her comic book. "And I think I'll call myself Cat Woman the Cat Burglar." She sat on the floor, the cat mask on top of her head with the elastic under her chin.

"I have to get into my role," said Lilah. "I have to stop thinking about Ruthie."

"It's hard to stop thinking," said Jilly. "Once, I tried and tried to stop thinking and I tried not to think about a purple hippopotamus and . . ."

"You can stop thinking about me now, girlfriends," said Ruthie, standing in the doorway. "Cuz I'm here."

CHAPTER EIGHTEEN

On With the Show

"Yay!" shouted Lilah and Jilly, jumping up and down. Ruthie was dressed in her black and red costume and had never looked so good.

"Shhhh," said Mrs. Krouch, peeking her head from the stage entrance. "Take your places, it's time for the last act . . . that's you," she hissed.

Mrs. Krouch's crankiness didn't bother Lilah at all. She felt like her heart had turned into a happy helium balloon that was rising up, up, up into the rafters. The balloon was filled with relief, excitement, and love for her friends all at the same time. Ruthie, all out of breath, threw her coat on a chair and grabbed the TV tray.

"I just need a minute," said Ruthie, catching her breath.

"You don't have a minute," said Mrs. Krouch. "Take your positions, NOW."

Lilah had to say one more thing for good luck. "Break a leg," she whispered to her friends, and they took their positions behind the curtain wings. Lilah peeked out, into the dark auditorium and could see that it was a full house. The bright stage lights prevented her from recognizing anyone in the audience, but she could tell there were lots of them when they applauded for Katrina, the dead swan.

Lilah gave Jilly the signal once Katrina had bowed and exited the stage with white feathers dropping behind her. Jilly pressed play, and the eerie theme music from "Star Trek" floated out into the audience.

Ruthie, looking flushed and a little sweaty, whispered, "Here, I brought you a surprise." She handed Lilah her top hat. It felt heavy. Lilah looked into the hat and saw a baby bunny.

"What?" she asked.

"I thought you could start by pulling a rabbit out of your hat," said Ruthie.

"But I never practiced that!"

The "Star Trek" music got very loud and Ruthie must have realized that she was late with her cue because she ran off, onto the stage with the TV tray, and put it in place. Then, she skipped back and forth, pulling scarves out of nowhere and tossing them into the air—so many that the audience let out an "ahhhh." The music faded and Ruthie took center stage.

"Presenting the one, the only, mystery woman, the, uh, the woman of illusion, the magician's magician, Lilah Dill, oops, no, um, the magician's magician . . . Shagundula." Ruthie put her right arm out, as Lilah had directed, and Lilah entered from stage right to the song "Do You Believe in Magic?."

CHAPTER NINETEEN

The Last Act

Lilah swept around the stage, swirling her cape this way and that, nodding and smiling to the audience. Her hat felt heavy and awkward. The bunny crouched low, keeping his balance on Lilah's head. This worried her, but she thought, *I'm already getting applause, just like I planned. If only my daddy could see me now.*

She stopped at center stage and put her hands up for quiet. Ruthie moved over to the TV tray, getting the first trick ready while the audience quieted down. Lilah could see Bongo and Jonny-cake sitting in the front row with a bunch of other little kids.

"Thank you for that wonderful welcome," Shagundula said. "Tonight, I will astound you with three illusions from the ages. But first, I'd like to take my hat off to you." *Here goes*, she thought.

Lilah bowed low and pulled her hat off of her head, attempting to scoop up the bunny, but the bunny hopped onto the stage and into the audience.

The entire front row jumped out of their seats in pursuit of the bunny. At first there were a few laughs and then there were more, and then there was actual hooting and guffawing as the bunny leaped and bounced out of the children's grasps.

Lilah froze with her hat in her hand.

Out of the corner of her eye she saw a flash of Hawaiian shirt near the floor. The house lights went up and Cornball Cloke held the bunny up in the air for everyone to see. The audience went wild with applause and whistles. Cornball, red-faced and grinning, gave a dramatic bow and then took it out through a side door.

The music stopped and Jilly peeked out from the back wing.

Mrs. Krouch and a few of the teachers came forth to herd the little kids back into their front row seats, and the audience settled down.

Lilah could hear her daddy's voice inside her head. It said, "The show must go on. You can do it, Lilah."

Lilah pushed her fear aside and

Shagundula took control. "Now that we have your attention, may we have the house lights dimmed?"

Miraculously, the auditorium lights went out and Lilah could once again feel the heat of the stage lights on her face. Happy music came back on with "Every Little Thing She Does is Magic." Lilah could picture Jilly, backstage, giving her the thumbs up.

Ruthie placed the TV tray in front of her and whispered, "Good save, Girlfriend."

The TV tray held three upside down silver cups with one green ball. Lilah introduced the trick and then placed the green ball under one of the cups. She then moved the cups around and looked at the front row.

"Little boy in the red shirt," she said, "Would you please point to the cup that hides the ball?"

The little boy pointed to the center cup. Lilah lifted it and there was no green ball to be seen. Each time she did this, the audience gasped in surprise. The ball wasn't where they thought it should be.

Just when Lilah thought things were going well, the green ball bounced off of the table, but Ruthie caught it and got it right back on the table. *Phew,* thought Lilah, *that was close.* She finished the trick with a bow and a jazzy little dance around the stage, gathering up the silk scarves, which appeared to disappear in her hands.

By the time she got back to center stage, Ruthie had removed the cups and replaced them with a three-sided screen.

Lilah opened her hands and displayed a long string of silk scarves, all tied together.

Applause, applause, applause.

Lilah stepped behind the TV tray, and handed the scarves to Ruthie, who waved them behind her, winked at the audience, and skipped off stage right.

"And now," Shagundula announced, "for the famous temple screen. As you can plainly see, these three attached screens can be folded flat, like a book, or upright, like a triangular box. Here it is flat, both sides, here a book. And now I will fold it into a triangle." She showed them the front and the back of the screens, and then demonstrated how the screens could be arranged in a standing triangle box shape.

"Oh! And what do we have here?" Shagundula pulled a bottle out of the triangle and then lifted the triangle and unfolded it to show that there was nothing hidden. She folded the screen again and this time she pulled out a bouquet of paper flowers.

Applause, applause, applause.

"And now," said Shagundula, "our last illusion, the famous floating ball." The music changed back to Star Trek. Ruthie and Jilly entered the stage carrying a big piece of striped velvet cloth.

Shagundula stood behind the cloth, put her hands high in the air and moved them with the music. The audience could see her legs, her head and her hands. A shiny silvery-blue ball appeared to float up from behind the cloth and around Shagundula's head. The audience went crazy.

The applause was thunderous. Lilah grabbed the cloth and the ball and took a deep bow. Ruthie and Jilly, blue cloth and ball in tow, exited stage right. The music changed back to "Do You Believe in Magic." The apprentice and the techie returned to the stage for their bows.

"And let's hear it," yelled Lilah, "for Ruthie Taylor and Jilly Frost, the best friends in the world." The audience rose to a standing ovation while all three girls held hands and took their bows.

Then, it looked as if the audience had split in two and Lilah could see something big and bright coming down the center aisle. It was her daddy!

Lilah's daddy handed her the biggest bouquet of red roses she had ever seen. A wide silver ribbon wrapped around them, ending in a big bow. "You were fabulous, Lilah. I'm so proud of you, and you did it all on your own." His eyes looked a little teary.

Lilah held the flowers close. "Thank you Daddy," she said "but I couldn't have done this without you to get me started, or without Ruthie and Jilly."

"That's what friends are for," said Jilly and Ruthie, full of big grins.

She handed each of the girls a rose.

By this time, the stage lights were dark and the house lights blazed white. Mrs. Krouch was at the microphone, trying to say something, but everyone was talking and moving and some were already leaving. Mrs. Krouch gave up and turned off the mic. "Thank you for coming and good night," she yelled.

CHAPTER 20

Lilah's Real Magic Kit

The next day found Lilah still feeling a glow from the night before. "I love Saturdays," she said, pumping with her legs so that she could get the swing higher. "Especially when my chores are all done."

"Me too," said Mama, looking up from a crossword puzzle. The thermometer said eighty-five degrees, but she sat at the shady end of the lanai with her feet up on a hassock.

"Me three," said Daddy, bringing a pitcher of lemonade and some plastic glasses out to the table. Old grass stains decorated the knees of his baggy pants. "How about you guys?" he called to the twins.

They were "watering the plants," but the little boys were wet, and the plants were dry.

"Me four," said Bongo.

"Me four too," said Jonny-cake.

Lilah slowed her swing and listened to Nana Belle playing "That Old Black Magic" on the piano in the living room. Nana had acted so proud of her and Ruthie and Jilly after the show, taking a little of the credit for herself, of course. It seemed like Showtime had happened weeks ago, not just the night before.

"Lilah, I can't get over how you pulled

that off last night," said her daddy. "Everyone is saying that it was the best act by far."

"Well, it was," said Mama. "Delilah's a chip off the old block."

Lilah's daddy smiled proudly.

"I meant my mother, you know," said Mama. She had a big grin on her face. "But you're not so bad yourself."

Daddy laughed. "Well, I've got to admit, Nana Belle is quite a pro." He stopped and listened to the piano music for a minute. "They both are," he added, smiling at Lilah.

"I liked the bunny," said Bongo, holding the hose. "Peter Rabbit. That's what his name is. Cornball told me."

"Where's Peter Rabbit now?" asked Jonny-cake.

"Oh," said Daddy. "Cornball found a nice home for him with other bunnies. He didn't want him to be lonely."

Bongo turned the hose on Jonny-cake who screamed with surprise and delight. Lilah slowed the swing to a stop and ran over to the bars, climbing into a position where she could hang from her knees. She loved her upside down world. "You know what?"

"What?" her upside-down mama and daddy asked.

"I think that I'm the luckiest girl in the whole universe."

"And why is that?" asked Mama.

Lilah pointed at each person in her family as she answered. "Because you and you and you and you and Nana Belle and Jilly and Ruthie and Cornball and the

Chicks are my real magic kit. The rest of the magic stuff is only tricks. I figured that out last night."

Her daddy had the biggest upside-down smile she had ever seen.

Theater Terms

Green Room: the room where the performers wait to go on stage . . . In the old days, when theaters were outside, performers waited behind the bushes and trees. That's why they call it the Green Room.

Back stage: behind the curtains or the stage

Break a leg: it's what you say to an actor right before they go on to wish them good luck.

Encore: an additional performance in response to a demand from an audience

Full House: all the audience seats are filled

Ovation: enthusiastic applause or cheering from a large group of people

Stage Directions

Stage Right: the right side of the stage, from the actor's point of view, looking at the audience

Stage Left: the left side of the stage

Center Stage: right smack in the middle of the stage

Down Stage: the part of the stage that's closest to the audience

Up Stage: the part of the stage that's the furthest from the audience

Wings: the curtains that come out from the sides of the stage

Musical Terms

Baritone: a man's singing voice that is lower than a tenor and higher than a bass

Duet: a pair of people singing together

Opera: a play where music is the most important part of the performance

Soprano: the highest singing voice

Acknowledgments

Thank you to my KidLit Café Critique group for your help and support in making this first chapter book happen. Also, thanks to Molly Woodward and Jo-Anne Rosen, for their wise advise and thoughtful editing and formatting, and to Edytha Ryan, whose illustrations helped Lilah's story come alive.

I'm particularly in debt to my loving but quirky family who provide endless material. Thank you all for a wonderful childhood. And lastly, thanks to the students and teachers of Carquinez and Cherry Valley Schools who inspired this book.

JEANNE (JL) JUSAITIS is the author of *Journey to Anderswelt*, a middle-grade fantasy set in Austria. Jeanne lives in Northern California, where, like Lilah, she started out in a little sugar town. She grew up to be a teacher of elementary school-aged children (which is almost like a magician) where she instilled the power of story writing and dramatics in her students. Her writing for young children is filled with humor. Mystery, mythology, friendship, and world travel are her themes when writing for young adults.

EDYTHA RYAN is a Northern California artist and writer whose illustrations capture the quirky quality of the Lilah Dill household. She artistically renders pandemonium in the last drawing of the book.

Order more copies of

Lilah Dill and the Magic Kit

at www.createspace.com/3952200

Also available from amazon.com
and other retailers.

Made in the USA
Charleston, SC
27 August 2012